"David Edwards is one of the b
knows the heartbeat of the cul
has done with this awesome bc
material and let others in on wl

He
he
iis

— JEFF LOVINGOOD, next ge

.. Baptist Church,
Hendersonville, Tennessee

"David Edwards has combined the passion of an evangelist and the teaching of a scholar in this book. In a time when students are biblically illiterate, David has called out a generation of students who will authentically pursue the mission of God found in the pages of Scripture. Students are looking for something to give their lives away to, and the raw meat of the Word of God is exactly what they have been looking for."

— SPENCER BARNARD, pastor to students, East Side Baptist Church,
Fort Smith, Arkansas

"What a great resource for helping students take in the Word and begin to live in it. First Book is the perfect name for these studies. The entire design makes *First Book Challenge* a great option for a small group of students as well as a great tool to build a weekend event around."

— RANDY HALL, CEO, Student Life

"Finally, a book that is radically committed to the Word of God and yet remains functionally practical. John Stamper brings his wealth of ministry experience to those who desire to follow the Lord Jesus Christ. John and David nail it in this book by presenting profound truth in a simplistic and action-oriented strategy."

— DR. DAVID E. ADAMS, executive director, International Center for Youth and
Family Ministry, Southern Baptist Theological Seminary and Boyce College

"After serving the local church the past thirty-eight years as a student pastor, there is no doubt in my mind that what is needed most in the hearts and lives of this generation is the Word of God. Anything that can help a student connect or reconnect with the Word of ‘God and His voice is worthy of my attention, time, and investment. *First Book Challenge* is powerful and effective, especially for such a time as this. It is the perfect resource for every teen, youth group, club, and home."

— PHIL NEWBERRY, campus pastor, Bellevue Arlington
Arlington, Tennessee

"I've watched kids change the course of their culture and make a difference for Christ on their campus using the principles that John and Dave teach using *First Book Challenge*. As a parent, I've benefited from my teens using the First Book message and methods. As a pastor, I've watched a groundswell of a movement that has changed homes and families. I'm eager to see God use this resource to change a generation."

— DR. RICHARD MARK LEE, senior pastor, First Baptist Church, McKinney, Texas

"David and John have made this simple for leaders of students. With *First Book Challenge*, not only are we creatively teaching the principles of God's Word in a unique way but we are also teaching students how to study the Scriptures for themselves. We plan to expose as many students as possible to this incredible new resource."

— GREG DAVIS, president, First Priority Ministry

"I've read the material, and all I can say is wow! There are books that impact a few lives, and then there are books like this one that alter churches, schools, cities, states, and nations! Dave Edwards has a track record of being a transformational author, and through *First Book Challenge*, he is at his best. Every student ministry in the country needs to take this journey."

— TONY NOLAN, speaker; author

"This is exactly what our students and adults need. Giving our students a handle to not only get in the Word but to get the Word in them is going to make an impact."

— MATTHEW CROWE, student pastor, First Baptist Church Black Forest, Colorado Springs, Colorado

A L I V E //

F I R S T B O O K C H A L L E N G E

EXPERIENCE THE
TRANSFORMATIONAL LIFE

DAVID EDWARDS • JOHN STAMPER

NAVPRESS
Discipleship Inside Out™

THINK

NavPress is the publishing ministry of The Navigators, an international Christian organization and leader in personal spiritual development. NavPress is committed to helping people grow spiritually and enjoy lives of meaning and hope through personal and group resources that are biblically rooted, culturally relevant, and highly practical.

For a free catalog go to www.NavPress.com or call 1.800.366.7788 in the United States or 1.800.839.4769 in Canada.

© 2011 by David Edwards and John Stamper

ISBN-13: 978-1-61747-166-7

Cover design by Faceout Studio
Cover image by Shutterstock
Author photos by Travis Clancy Photography, Edmond, OK

Some of the anecdotal illustrations in this book are true to life and are included with the permission of the persons involved. All other illustrations are composites of real situations, and any resemblance to people living or dead is coincidental.

Unless otherwise identified, all Scripture quotations in this publication are taken from the New American Standard Bible® (NASB). Copyright © 1960, 1962, 1963, 1968, 1971, 1972, 1973, 1975, 1977, 1995 by The Lockman Foundation. Used by permission. Other versions used include: the *Holy Bible, New International Version*® (NIV®). Copyright © 1973, 1978, 1984 by International Bible Society. Used by permission of Zondervan. All rights reserved; the New King James Version (NKJV). Copyright © 1982 by Thomas Nelson, Inc. Used by permission. All rights reserved; and the King James Version (KJV).

Printed in the United States of America

1 2 3 4 5 6 7 8 / 16 15 14 13 12 11

CONTENTS

FOREWORD

Can I feel God? Is there any way I can find an answer to my personal crises? What do I do about my relationships? These, along with many others, are questions that students are asking the church and the student ministry to answer. Sadly, the answers they hear from pulpits and platforms are often emotionally centered, not compelling, and lacking enough content and substance to make a difference in the way students answer the questions of life and deal with their drama. What results from this is students leave the church in search of better answers. Something crucial is missing.

The priority and the use of Scripture have almost disappeared for many. Often the Word of God is no longer a part of church service and student night. It has been de-elevated. The tragic result is that students are trying to answer their questions, deal with their problems, and take on life without reliable truth. We have a generation of students whose identity is defined by whatever one needs it to be and wherever one happens to find it.

God never intended our lives to be lived this way. Scripture points us to a creative God of Truth and a loving Savior. The Bible can be trusted. I thank God for the First Book Challenge and what it will mean to students. In a culture where the Bible is readily available, the key is to present answers in a relevant way that grips the heart and mind. The First Book Challenge helps students know how to interact with Scripture and make God's Book their First Book.

The First Book Challenge is compelling. It teaches students how to not only understand God's Word but also live it out in relationships. The information in this three-book series is powerful and will impact the way people do life. One part of the First Book Challenge is that each student would receive a Bible to study as part of this series and then give a Bible away to a friend who doesn't have one — that is good news! I believe that by getting students into the Word and the Word into the life of students, we can see a cultural change in the home, school, and church. I am thrilled for you and your student ministry to take the First Book Challenge!

JOSH McDOWELL
writer, researcher, speaker

THE FIRST BOOK CHALLENGE

In those days the word of the LORD was rare.
1 SAMUEL 3:1 (NIV)

In Samuel's day, the Word of God was not spoken, read, or heard. It had been devalued. Samuel's world was a *wordless* one until, as a young student, he was trained to listen.

The same is true of our world. We live in a quickly changing culture. Shifting values produce self-stylized spirituality and a search for self-fulfillment. It would be easy to assign the blame to music, art, entertainment, or government, but the truth is that a clear grounding in the Word of God has been removed from the landscape of society. The shockwaves of a wordless society caused by the disappearance of the Word of God have resulted in the removal of school prayer, the visible absence of the Ten Commandments, and blurred lines between right and wrong. As you face these changes, you find yourself living in a world of moral gray areas evidenced by the rise of social drinking, the decline of moral boundaries, a loss of respect for others, a heightened sense of entitlement, and a driving belief that people are only a means to an end. Access to the Word of God is not the problem. Bibles fill the lost-and-found boxes in many churches. What *is* lacking is a personal connection to God's Word accompanied by skills to understand and use the Bible.

Without a working knowledge of Scripture, you will lose your grasp on God's Word. This releases a chain reaction of anger and resentment, which leads to lack of purpose and disappointment with life. Losing your grasp on God's Word and truth makes it more likely that you will steal, be abusive to others, cheat on an exam, use illegal drugs, attempt suicide, or participate in other physically, emotionally, or spiritually destructive behaviors. The Bible is the change agent for this generation. A deeply held belief in God and His Word will serve as the foundation of your faith so that no matter what comes your way, you can stand strong. God has always been speaking, even in Samuel's day. The Word of God still speaks. The question for us today is, "Who is listening?"

There is a generation of students who refuse to listen to the prevailing voice of society and its relentless pursuit of materialism. They will no longer be led astray by easy "believe-ism" but instead have embraced God's standard of absolute truth and the pursuit of godliness. They have heard the call to continue holding on to the priority of Scripture, believing that the Word of God proclaims salvation for all. They believe the Bible is not a textbook but the very revelation of Christ, who is our hope for eternal life. The Bible uniquely unlocks the true identity, purpose, and destiny of our lives. It assures us that God has not left us alone to grope our way through life but has given us His wisdom in His Word to be studied, believed, and obeyed. This is a generation that is pursuing biblical faith, is rooted and grounded in God's Word, and speaks with conviction the truths of Scripture. These students have set their lives in motion by His Spirit. They have picked up His Book and made it their First Book. What will you do?

"CHEAT SHEET" FOR FIRST BOOK CHALLENGE

This is not an endorsement of dishonesty but a helpful summary of the sections found in the four chapters of this book. Understanding the structure of each chapter will help you more effectively encounter God through Scripture.

We hope that as you accept the First Book Challenge, you will encounter God and His Word in a fresh way. Each chapter is made up of seven sections to help you experience His Word and the life He has for you:

Principle: This is the big idea phrased in a brief and memorable way—one thing you should be able to take away from the chapter and apply to your relationship with God. The principle is the hook on which the truth of the chapter hangs. The principle is meant to be memorable, understandable, and doable.

Passage: This is the passage of Scripture referenced throughout the chapter. Often Bible studies are filled with multiple references from different books of the Bible that require the reader to skip from book to book looking at the verses without much chance to absorb the content. Each chapter will explain the truth behind one passage with the intention of helping you encounter God and His Word. Make sure you have a Bible and pen with you while reading *First Book Challenge*. Visit www.firstbookchallenge.org for Bible resources and journals.

Unpacking the Passage: This section provides a list of questions that will help you internalize the Scripture and gain a sense of the message behind each passage. These questions are designed to get you to think about the text at a deeper level. Exhaustive responses are not required, just an opportunity to allow God's Word to stir your senses.

Off the Page: Reading Scripture can sometimes be challenging, especially in a culture of texting and tweeting. We all learn differently. Some think in facts and figures, while others think in pictures. This section provides new and buoyant ways to encounter Scripture and make it a part of your heart, mind, and soul.

Personal Download: Reading or hearing Scripture can be difficult when you don't see how it applies to your life. Studying the Bible involves more than just gathering information. It is through the steady act of applying Scripture that the reader reaches a deeper level of understanding. This section will lead you to take the passage and see how it applies to your personal environment, your circumstances, and the current choices you may be facing. In this section, you will view Scripture through the lenses of your life.

Live the Word: This section highlights students who have lived out the principles of Scripture by choosing to make God's Book their First Book. These are true stories of students who have faced struggles and challenges and have seen God do incredible things in their lives. These are encouraging stories, demonstrating how God and His Word cause amazing things to happen.

Heart Challenge: After each student's story, you will be challenged to respond directly and honestly to a few questions. These questions will allow you to reflect on how God is speaking and moving in your life. This section prods you to answer the question "What are you going to do about it?" Parts of these Bible studies may help you recognize that you are the answer to someone else's need. Your answer to God will determine the way in which you will respond to the First Book Challenge.

INTRODUCTION

I first noticed the problem when I was entering the store. I pushed the door to open it when the sign on the door clearly read, "Pull." I saw the sign just seconds after my face encountered the door. It occurred to me that I might need an eye exam.

I scheduled an appointment with my optometrist. If you haven't been to the eye doctor in a while, here's how it works: They start by putting you in a really cold and dark room. Then they put your face in front of a contraption that looks like some sort of medieval torture device. Air is shot into your eyes, followed by the doctor asking, "Can you see?" (I respond, "No, Doc, not now. You shot air into my eyes!") Next comes the eye chart: a giant board with letters printed in descending order from font size 96 all the way down to 6. You read the letters out loud. The first line is "E." (At this point I think, *I've got it.*)

For me, the second line didn't seem too difficult. I read all the letters from left to right. By the third line, I asked the doctor, "Can I buy a vowel?" For the next portion of the exam, I was instructed to sit behind a pair of giant goggles made up of multiple lenses and gears. I looked like a bionic fly. As the doctor flipped the lenses, he asked, "Better like this or like that? Better like one or like two?" As he went through the process, the teeny-tiny letters would come into view. I would say, "Yes, I can see now." Needless to say, the doc determined I needed glasses, and now I can read the signs on doors! My vision has improved, but the glasses are *another* thing to keep up with (and try not to break).

Just as eyeglasses help bring objects into focus, the four chapters of this book are designed to bring one truth into focus: You can encounter God through Scripture. These chapters are designed to inspire, encourage, and invite you to read God's Book. Why is this so important? Because for most students, their whole understanding of the Bible is made up of a few stories they remember from Sunday school and the sermons they listen to in church. In fact, most people know very little about the Bible. Their understanding is fuzzy at best.

How can you determine what you know about the Bible? Well, you might not know much about the Bible if:

- You think a concordance is a type of fine china dinnerware.
- You think having a leather-bound Bible makes you more spiritual (and that writing in it makes God mad at you).
- When first hearing about the New Testament, you ask, "When is it coming out?" because you really like sequels.
- You believe that Santa knelt by the baby Jesus, right between the shepherd and the sheep.
- You think the minor prophets were called "minor" because they were all under twenty-one.
- You believe that apostle, apostasy, and apocrypha all mean the same thing.
- You think part of the resurrection story includes Jesus coming out of the tomb, seeing His shadow, and then going back inside for three days.
- You think Pontius was the pilot during the "flight to Egypt."
- You think Genesis is about baseball ("In the *big inning* . . .").
- You think Daniel played tennis (*"serving* in Nebuchadnezzar's court").
- You think "Passover" is a football term.
- You've tried to find the street you live on in the map section in the back.

- You need a thumb-indexed Bible to find the book of Genesis.
- You think your Bible's part of the LEFT BEHIND series.
- You have read only three parts: your name, who gave it to you, and the verse that says, "Wives, submit to your husbands" (if you're male).
- Your favorite verse is "God helps those who help themselves."

So, what's the deal with the Bible? It's much more than a collection of stories that we've heard. It's also much more than a historical account or selection of the Wisdom Literature, and it bypasses the label of children's stories. The Bible is meant to be used in our relationship with God to bring about transformation in our lives.

I often have the same conversation with students in churches all over the country: "I don't feel God anymore. I keep praying and nothing happens. I just really want to feel the presence of God. What else can I do?" When I ask them if they read their Bible, they quickly reply that they don't. That response is always followed by excuses for not reading Scripture. Some say they don't know where to start. Others don't believe they can understand it; they assume that teachers, pastors, and Christian motivational speakers are the only ones who can explain it, so they settle for having someone else tell them what Scripture is saying. The Bible is too important to be left in the hands of "experts." God has given us His words as a way to experience His work.

Other students own dust-covered Bibles; they think the Bible has nothing relevant to say to their lives, so they don't crack it open. Some refuse to read it, believing it to be full of errors. Some set the Bible aside out of denial; they don't want to think about what they are doing with their lives. Still others say they already have a grasp on right and wrong and therefore don't need any help from God. But what is the biggest reason people don't read their Bibles? They just don't make time for it.

God's Word is living and active to those who read it. The Bible comes alive and speaks. It has much to say regarding the life God desires for us to live though Him. The Bible is the means by which we connect to the thought, emotions, and will of God. He invites us to experience the rush of His Word *becoming* His Word to us. As you read Scripture, you will quickly discover that the words of Scripture are alive. There is nothing you'll face in life that the Bible in some way does not already address. When life is out of focus, finding answers to problems can be difficult. But the Bible speaks to our feelings and the issues we face.

Regardless of what you face in life and what you feel in those moments, God's Word will help. The Bible is alive, and in every chapter and verse, God is directly communicating with you. In these four sessions, you will discover the dangers of not knowing God's Word, the benefits of knowing God's Word, how to connect the Word of God to specific thoughts in your mind, and the strategy for making God's Word the present force in your life. Now let's get started.

CHAPTER 1

CAN I GET A LITTLE HELP HERE?

PRINCIPLE:
KNOW BEFORE YOU GO.

Last year I made a life choice that will haunt me for years to come. I went against my better judgment and followed the crowd, right into a sandpile in the middle of nowhere, in Possumneck, Mississippi. (That really is the name of the town. Google it.) I, the most technologically challenged person you will ever know, took the advice of my techie nerd friends and bought a GPS for my car. These friends convinced me that the GPS would radically change my traveling experiences. "Everyone has one," they taunted. "You'll wonder how you ever lived without it." I succumbed to the hype. This was a terrible mistake.

In keeping with the GPS owner code, I named my GPS. Her name was Kate because she had the nicest British accent, and every girl I have ever met (or watched in a movie) from Great Britain is named Kate. When traveling to a new destination, I would normally call ahead and ask for an e-mail or fax of the directions, but not this time. I had my girl Kate, and Kate was going to lead me straight to First Baptist Church with no problem. I didn't even bring my road atlas.

At first Kate was so charming and calm. She spoke with the ease of a seasoned veteran. I could picture her in magical GPS land: feet propped up on her desk, sipping on her Starbucks, telling me, "Dave, I've got this. Just do what I say and you'll arrive safely with time to spare." But Kate was a conniving, lying sack of dirt and worms—that's what Kate was. And when I didn't follow her directions exactly, she turned on me like bad Mexican food.

I took the exit Kate told me to take. And I kept driving just like she instructed, until she told me to take a right on a street that was not a street but a path where I was likely to run into Hansel and Gretel. This is where I took matters into my own hands. I made the executive decision to override Kate and make a U-turn. Bad idea. Sweet, gentle Kate quickly lost her sanity. She started panicking and yelling, "Recalculating! Recalculating!" I shouted in return, "Okay, okay, get a hold of yourself, Kate!"

This is when Kate decided to get even with me. She started telling me to turn every mile or so onto roads that were either imaginary or so full of potholes that I ended up driving on the shoulder or the median. She directed me to turn too early and then yelled at me when I desperately obeyed her. "RECALCULATING!!! RECALCULATING!!!" She yelled at me as if I were the one ruining her day. It dawned on me that I was witnessing the tragedy of the complete nervous breakdown of my GPS. This went on and on until, out of nowhere, Kate became eerily calm again. "Turn left in point-five miles," she cooed. I did. "Your destination is point-seven miles on the right." I looked to the right and thought, This giant sandpile is a really strange place to have church. Can I get a little help here?

///////////

Many times on our Christian journey, we end up in similar situations. We listen to well-meaning people who are so willing to tell us how to get to where we want to go. We listen to the coolest speakers. We read the latest books. And before we know it, we are looking at a big pile of sand, thinking, *This is not where I meant to end up.* Everybody has an opinion about how to handle life. Friends, family members, singers, and movie stars always have advice and insight to offer: "Do what you want. Do what seems right to you. All is fair in love and war." All these voices start to run together. It's like doing an Internet search for a single subject and being bombarded with a thousand different options. The problem is that we take directions from a variety of sources but neglect the most reliable Source. Think of the Bible as the most accurate GPS available to take you where God wants you to be. Scripture must be your primary source for direction.

The Word of God has always had a lasting impact from one generation to the next. It's likely that the book from which Joshua read was the identical manuscript Moses wrote in the wilderness. The same book appeared a thousand years after Joshua's leadership during the reign of Josiah and then again in the book of Ezra as he read the book aloud in the street, making God's Word clear to the people who heard. The *Word* of God has always directed the *people* of God to their destiny. God tells Joshua many times to be "strong and courageous" (for example, 1:6). This is not a reference to his character. Joshua was a great man. This is a reference to his actions. The book of Joshua opens with the death of Moses and with Joshua as the new leader of Israel. Joshua faced the biggest challenge of his life. There would be battles to fight and conflicts to resolve while facing the unknown. Joshua needed the confidence that he was making the right decisions. He decided on the steps he would take after meditating on God's Word. For Joshua to face all of his enemies while dealing with Israel's numerous meltdowns, he would have to study God's Word.

⬤ PASSAGE:
JOSHUA 1:7-9

Be strong and very courageous. Be careful to obey all the law my servant Moses gave you; do not turn from it to the right or to the left, that you may be successful wherever you go. Do not let this Book of the Law depart from your mouth; meditate on it day and night, so that you may be careful to do everything written in it. Then you will be prosperous and successful. Have I not commanded you? Be strong and courageous. Do not be terrified; do not be discouraged, for the LORD your God will be with you wherever you go. (NIV)

God told Joshua to meditate on His Word day and night. It was to be in his thoughts and in the words he spoke at all times. Joshua's day was to begin with God's Word, and he would carry that Word into his tasks and struggles. At the end of his day, while he read the Word of God, he was to think back to the challenges he had faced that day. The next morning, he would begin again with the Word of God.

Meditating on God's Word does not mean going into a trance, endlessly chanting, or daydreaming. To meditate means to focus your mind, will, and emotions on Scripture with the intent of living out the truths of God's Word. The Bible is a powerful book that contains lessons on how to handle life's situations. It contains doctrine that shapes our understanding of God, Jesus, the church, and the future of the world. Within the pages of Scripture are great stories and word pictures of profound insight simple enough for a child to understand and yet so deep that readers of all ages are challenged. The content of Scripture is vast yet compact enough to be remembered and provide direction.

> There are many purposes of Scripture. One of these is to provide wisdom so we will know what to do.

There are many purposes of Scripture. One of these is to provide wisdom so we will know what to do. All of us have had moments in our lives when we have made an instant decision without asking anybody, without praying, and without consulting God's Word. There is no way to truly understand how important God's Word is in our lives until we look at the consequences of leaving God's Word out of our decision-making process. The book of Joshua records the battles he fought to take Israel into the Promised Land. Joshua faced intimidating forces and opposing obstacles but steadily overcame each one of them with God's Word as his source of guidance.

The spectacular victories of Joshua over Jericho and the city of Ai caused the Canaanites to fear Israel's strength as an army. The next city in Joshua's path was Gibeon, which was situated northwest of Jerusalem and opposite the valley of Ai.

The Gibeonites devised a plan to survive Joshua's attack. They disguised themselves as refugees because they knew that if Joshua recognized them, they would face certain danger. They came to Joshua dressed as weary travelers, wearing old clothes and carrying only a few pieces of moldy food. They asked Joshua to take them in and protect them. They convinced Joshua that they believed in God, and he promised to protect them.

One of the elements that adds to the Bible's reliability is that it shows its heroes making unwise decisions, struggling, and failing. The story in Joshua 9 takes a dramatic turn when Joshua "did not ask for the counsel of the LORD" (verse 14). What follows in this story are the consequences of Joshua's acting before getting God's go-ahead.

1. When you make decisions on your own without knowing God's Word, **you can expect to be royally scammed**. Joshua overestimated his ability to control the outcome of situations: "These wineskins which we filled were new, and behold, they are torn" (Joshua 9:13). Making a decision based solely on how things look overestimates your own ability. You reason, *It looks good to me! Nothing bad is going to happen. How*

could I mess this one up? How often do you make the same mistake? Do you ever think of yourself more highly than you should? You have probably looked at a seemingly simple decision and wondered how you could mess up something so easy. After all, it's an easy choice; what could go wrong? You've thought it through, right? It seems like a good idea, so you go for it. But when you look in the rearview mirror of experience, you see how completely wrong you were.

We mistakenly believe what we see instead of trusting what God knows. Instead of taking the time and putting in the effort to check out our decision with God, we put confidence in our own judgment. We forget that God's thoughts are higher than ours and that His ways far exceed our understanding. He *is* wisdom and the source of all truth and knowledge. His wisdom, truth, and knowledge are available to anyone who will simply ask Him for insight into His will.

2. Removing the Word of God from your life reduces you to having to **rely on your own senses**. Joshua made the decision based on what he saw: "These our clothes and our sandals are worn out because of the very long journey" (verse 13). How many times have you thought, *Hey, it looks good to me. What could go wrong?* Don't do this. Anytime you rely on your senses — no matter how sharp they may seem — you can expect to be misled. You may have made several good decisions that have worked out okay, but sooner or later you will be misled, and that will likely come at the most inappropriate time.

> Unless we know what God's Word has to say specifically to us, we should not move forward.

God has a will for the details of our lives, not just for the big events. We can get all the data that's available, using every sensory perception technique known to man, but unless we know what God's Word has to say specifically to us, we should not move forward. It doesn't matter how perceptive we are — if all we are using is our senses, in the end we're just guessing. We can take advantage of all the human counsel available, but without a word from God, we will be misled.

I've talked with countless young women who are certain that the guy they want to date is just one character trait removed from filling the shoes of the Antichrist. They ask me if they should date him. I ask them if they know what the Word of God has to say about dating him. They respond that they know how bad he is, but they're going to date him anyway. You can guarantee that the peace of God will not be on that relationship. In relationships and other areas of thinking, many make the mistake of thinking that they can do anything they choose, and when things go bad, they can call out to God and He'll bail them out. Sorry. It doesn't work that way.

3. Making decisions without knowing the Word of God means **you have missed the check of the Spirit of God**. The leaders Joshua had around him were suspicious of these disguised Gibeonites. They did not believe the Gibeonites, but Joshua would not listen: "The men of Israel said . . . 'Perhaps you are living within our land'" (verse 7). God uses the voices of your leaders, advisers, and counselors (to name a few) to let you know you need to be careful before you make a mistake. God's Word says that there is wisdom in a multitude of counselors. God uses parents, friends, and church leaders to bring you into check before you make a mistake. But sometimes you are so locked in on a choice that you don't listen. It looks like a great decision, but do you have God's permission?

When we find ourselves in the worst-possible situations, we sometimes reject logical advice. God sends friends to tell us that when we get into certain situations, we don't act like ourselves. But instead of listening to their advice, we do what we want to do. God is our Ultimate Friend when we are about to make a wrong decision. This is called "a check in our spirits." Down deep in our hearts, we know that something isn't right.

When the check in the spirit comes, it is time to seek God's counsel. It's time to delay making the decision until talking things over with God. When we do, He makes the full measure of His infinite wisdom available to us. His wisdom is always right; it can always be trusted.

4. Without God's wisdom, the **decisions we make will result in constant struggle**. The agreement Joshua made with the Gibeonites became a point of attack. It resulted in a high-maintenance situation that

took all of Joshua's resources to turn it around: "Do not abandon your servant; come up to us quickly and save us and help us. . . . So Joshua went . . . he and all the people of war with him and all the valiant warriors" (10:6-7). If we move forward without getting God's okay, a bad situation gets worse; we get entangled in the fallout of that bad choice and fight

> **We know God's Word by reading God's Word. It's just that simple.**

unnecessary battles. It's one thing to be in a fight because we are following God's instruction and doing the right thing. It's quite another thing to be in a fight because we've made a decision apart from God's wisdom. When we live in God's wisdom, we can count on His limitless resources to be available for every situation we face. When we operate outside of God's wisdom and will, we can only expect to draw on our own limited resources. If you're anything like me, you'd probably rather face a fight inside the will of God with His eternal resources at work than stand defenseless in the face of the smallest battle.

So when we find ourselves in these situations, what are we to do? How are we to handle tough decisions? There is only one remedy for dealing with these situations: reading Scripture. We know God's Word by reading God's Word. It's just that simple.

We make decisions every day. Some of these decisions are life changing, while others seem to have little impact. Regardless of how these decisions appear, we must learn that the Word of God affects every area, not just one. Every facet of our lives is affected by the will of God. Every decision we are faced with requires a clear knowledge and understanding of God's Word. Here are three suggestions to help you get a clear direction from Scripture.

• **Read the Bible systematically.** Don't take a single verse out of context. Some people read the Bible by randomly looking at verses in different parts of the Bible. Reading in bits and pieces is okay if you are reading a magazine, but it is a mistake when studying the Bible. It creates a fragmented sense of Scripture that lacks depth. A far better way is to read books of the Bible from beginning to end at one time. A new

Christian could begin with one of the Gospels, while someone who has been a believer for some time might start with Romans. It's a good idea to read each book twice. The first read-through gives you a sense of the story as a whole: how it starts, what's in the middle, and how it ends. The second reading is for details: what's being said, why it's being said, and who is saying it. By reading systematically, you will experience the God of Scripture. It is at this point that the Holy Spirit causes the Word of God to become personal. Going through this process allows you to know what God is saying. Once you understand the context, take it into consideration. Understand the big picture before you act on what you believe God is saying.

> Every decision we are faced with requires a clear knowledge and understanding of God's Word.

• **Use a pen and a highlighter.** Ask God to help you understand what you are reading. The Bible is God's Word. It comes from God's mind — the same mind that created the world and everything in it. Ask Him. He'll tell you what He means. Highlight words, phrases, and verses you want to understand better. Write notes in the margins. Write questions you have about the text.

• **Read the Bible with sensitivity.** Ask the Holy Spirit to apply the Scripture to your life. Suddenly you'll not only understand what God's Word means but also understand what it means for your life.

UNPACKING THE PASSAGE

1. What does God tell Joshua at this point in his life when he is being called to pick up where Moses left off and lead the nation of Israel?

2. What does God mean when He says that Joshua "will be prosperous and successful"? Compare and contrast the Old Testament meaning with today's meaning.

3. How is it possible to "meditate on [Scripture] day and night"? What does this mean?

4. According to Joshua 1:8, what is the number one requirement to experience prosperity and success?

OFF THE PAGE

Meditate means to focus with the intent to act with purpose. First-rate Bible reading calls not for snapshots but for timed exposures in high definition. It requires focused attention on God's Word over long periods of time. At the onset of Joshua's new leadership responsibility, God told him to focus on His Word and that the benefits would follow. When we meditate on Scripture, we allow a specific place in our lives to converge with it. We allow the truth of God's Word to bear down on problem areas, and when it does, the clutter is removed and creates room for us to know the wisdom of God.

Get your think on. When you read Scripture, don't just *look* at the words. Instead, *think* about what you're reading. Give it the same amount of concentration you would give to playing a computer game, learning a foreign language, or solving a math problem. Reading the Bible is not like glancing at a magazine. The Bible's message is beneath the surface, so you have to study, investigate, and ask questions of it. As you read the text of Scripture, it is helpful to ask specific questions, such as:

- Why is this included in the Bible?
- What issue, whether personal or social, does it speak to?
- What is the one revolutionary thought in this text?

Digging into God's Word and asking these types of questions will help you find better answers.

PERSONAL DOWNLOAD

Reread Joshua 1:7-9, the chapter's passage. The following questions and suggestions for memorization will help you apply the principle of this chapter to your life and strengthen your journey toward being more like Christ.

1. What do you think Joshua was feeling at the time of Moses' death as he was taking over the leadership of Israel?

2. Describe a time in your life when you felt alone and scared in response to being asked to do something for God.

3. Why is it so difficult to "do everything" written in Scripture?

4. God knew Joshua's emotional state and continuously encouraged him. What kind of impact does this have on you?

5. Commit Joshua 1:8 to memory. The verse will remind you of God's promise that you will receive true prosperity and success — not according to the world's temporary and empty standards — when you meditate on His Word.

///

💬 LIVE THE WORD

Maturity is not based on age; it is based on action. It's based on what you *do* with your knowledge of Scripture — how you encounter God and whether you decide to allow that encounter to stay filed away in your head or lead you to become who you were created to be.

Chris was a young man who accepted Christ when he was in the fifth grade. Christ became real to him. His relationship with Jesus became more than head knowledge or a simple religious icon to worship. Christ became a part of his life. A true and radical transformation took place in this young man. It was at this point that Chris decided he wanted to do something with his life. He committed to not only make a splash but also create a huge tidal wave in his relationships. After attending a leadership event, he wrote down his dreams and aspirations.

Chris decided that he was going to make an impact on his school. He committed to *externally* sharing the God whom he had already experienced and encountered *internally*. He wanted to share the life God had given him. The first step he took was to get direction from God's Word. Chris began reading the first chapter of Joshua. His eyes fell on verse 3, "I will give you every place where you set your foot" (NIV). At that very moment, he knew that God was giving him the green light to begin a campus ministry. Chris shared with a school leader the vision God had given him to impact his school. He wanted to launch a club focused on sharing Scripture and encountering God in a way most students had never experienced. His leader told Chris that as an adult, he would not be allowed to help in any way other than unlocking the door. As you can imagine, this was somewhat deflating to Chris. However, Chris believed what God had shown him in Joshua and decided to continue with his dream. Chris opened his Bible and read Joshua 1 again. As his mind soaked in the phrase "meditate on it day and night . . . and then you will have success" (verse 8), he knew that God was assuring him that the plan would work if he started it the way God wanted. Chris held on to this verse as God's confirmation to go ahead.

Chris launched his club. His first year, in sixth grade, Chris had about thirty-five students coming weekly. Several came to know Christ and became regular club members. At the end of his seventh-grade year, Chris witnessed the growth of the vision God had placed in his heart. At the end of the year, nearly a hundred students were attending meetings every week. Students were baptized as witnesses to their new lives in Christ. At the close of his eighth-grade year, Chris was averaging close to three hundred peers attending every week. Students opened the Word of God and worshipped in authenticity. More than fifty students were baptized. The club had gone from meeting in a small classroom to meeting in the gym. All this started with a fifth-grade boy who allowed God to use him so others could encounter Christ.

Go to www.firstbookchallenge.org to tell us your story about how God and His Word have made a difference in your life, friends, family, school, and church.

///

 HEART CHALLENGE

Are you willing to be so bold as to do something about the dreams and convictions God has placed in your life? Make today the day that you begin to live out loud for Christ. Don't wait until tomorrow to become all God created you to be.

1. Write down what God is saying to you. Express in written words what He has placed on your heart.

2. List specific steps you will take to act on God's Word in your life. Write names of individuals you can impact with the truth of God's Word.

3. Ask God to open doors for you. Ask Him to give you the strength to become all you were created to be. Pray that God will press you to boldly live out His call on your life.

WRITE COOL STUFF HERE

WRITE COOL STUFF HERE

CHAPTER 2

THE NEED TO READ

PRINCIPLE:
YOU CAN'T QUOTE IT IF YOU DON'T KNOW IT.

The Bible was not divided into chapters and verses until hundreds of years after the individual books were written. This was done as an effort to help users reference it. Before chapters and verses were added, Sunday schools might have sounded something like this: "Find the book of Romans. Now look somewhere near the beginning at the sentence starting with, 'For all have sinned.' No, Sam, you've gone too far. It's kind of near the middle of the page — well, at least that's where it is in my Bible." When everyone literally got on the same page, the bell would ring, summoning everyone to Big Church. Now, imagine how long it would have taken everyone to get on the same page in Big Church!

Chapters and verses are like addresses for a house: They help you locate sections of Scripture and keep you from saying, "I don't know where it is, but I think it says . . ." Chapters and verses also give you an idea of the flow and order of thought. They create the context for Scripture and help you locate specific passages when you need them.

Sometimes Scripture, when taken out of context, make for some pretty hilarious memory verses for anything you may experience:

- For when your siblings are annoying you: "Behold, I will corrupt your seed, and spread dung up on your faces." (Malachi 2:3, KJV)
- For when the guy you met on Facebook is boring in real life: "Some say, 'His letters are weighty and forceful, but in person he is unimpressive and his speaking amounts to nothing.'" (2 Corinthians 10:10, NIV)
- For the worst first date ever: "All tables are full of vomit and filthiness, so that there is no place clean." (Isaiah 28:8, KJV)
- For when you want a reason to have one more Kit Kat: "He that is of a proud heart stirreth up strife: but he that putteth his trust in the LORD shall be made fat." (Proverbs 28:25, KJV)
- For when you have to defeat the martians: "Quenched the violence of fire, escaped the edge of the sword, out of weakness were made strong, waxed valiant in fight, turned to flight the armies of the aliens." (Hebrews 11:34, KJV)
- For when the preacher is too long-winded: "There was a young man named Eutychus sitting on the window sill, sinking into a deep sleep; and as Paul kept on talking, he was overcome by sleep and fell down from the third floor and was picked up dead." (Acts 20:9)
- For eating raw oysters: "Let's swallow them alive, like the grave, and whole, like those who go down to the pit." (Proverbs 1:12, NIV)

As you can see, committing Scripture to memory can be helpful in any situation. But you can't quote it if you don't know it!

/ / / / / / / / / / /

Life doesn't happen in a vacuum. When it comes to living life and following God, things can get messy. We can get worn out from the workload of school, the expectations of others, the drama at home, and all the emotions we experience at once as our lives get busier and more complicated. The stresses of life can affect our sleep, health, and thinking. When you start to feel stressed out, look out! That is when the Enemy likes to attack and get you to make unwise choices and do things you would not ordinarily do.

You are not alone in facing tough times; Jesus also faced them in His life. There was a time when He was tired and hungry and emotionally drained. Matthew records how the Enemy came to tempt Him in hopes of pulling Him away from what He had come to earth to do. However, Jesus knew what it took to defeat temptation. Not once did He ever let the Enemy get the best of Him, as Jesus knew one important thing: how to quote Scripture at the right time and right place. Now, let me ask you one simple question: If Jesus had to quote the Bible in order to fight temptation, how much more should we?

We must know what the Bible says about the issues that we are dealing with so that the Word can infiltrate our circumstances, thoughts, and behavior. The Word of God keeps us from falling for every temptation thrown at us. It's always been the battle plan of Jesus. Knowing God's Word in the midst of our daily demands is what gets us through those times. In this session, we are going to look at the role the Bible played in the life of Jesus. It is interesting to see in Scripture that Jesus thought the Old Testament was divinely inspired and made references to it as the Word of God.

We must know what the Bible says about the issues that we are dealing with so that the Word can infiltrate our circumstances, thoughts, and behavior.

PASSAGE:
MATTHEW 4:1–11

Then Jesus was led up by the Spirit into the wilderness to be tempted by the devil. And after He had fasted forty days and forty nights, He then became hungry.

And the tempter came and said to Him, "If You are the Son of God, command that these stones become bread."

But He answered and said, "It is written, 'MAN SHALL NOT LIVE ON BREAD ALONE, BUT ON EVERY WORD THAT PROCEEDS OUT OF THE MOUTH OF GOD.'"

Then the devil took Him into the holy city and had Him stand on the pinnacle of the temple, and said to Him, "If You are the Son of God, throw Yourself down; for it is written,

'HE WILL COMMAND HIS ANGELS CONCERNING YOU';

and

'ON THEIR HANDS THEY WILL BEAR YOU UP,
SO THAT YOU WILL NOT STRIKE YOUR FOOT AGAINST A STONE.'"

Jesus said to him, "On the other hand, it is written, 'YOU SHALL NOT PUT THE LORD YOUR GOD TO THE TEST.'"

Again, the devil took Him to a very high mountain and showed Him all the kingdoms of the world and their glory; and he said to Him, "All these things I will give You, if You fall down and worship me."

Then Jesus said to him, "Go, Satan! For it is written, 'YOU SHALL WORSHIP THE LORD YOUR GOD, AND SERVE HIM ONLY.'"

Then the devil left Him; and behold, angels came and began to minister to Him.

The Word of God speaks to our needs and works to bring freedom into our lives in three very specific ways:

Serves as the antidote to temptation: "tempted by the devil" (Matthew 4:1). Scripture is the only remedy for temptation. Scripture dilutes the effects temptation has on our minds and makes it resistible. Knowing Scripture will allow us to conquer the desire of sin and refuse temptation the next time it comes our way.

Here's an example of how Jesus used the Word when He faced temptation. In Matthew 4:1-11, the Spirit of God led Jesus into the wilderness to be tempted by Satan. When Satan came to Jesus, he dared Him to prove He had all the messianic power. If Jesus had made bread out of stones, jumped off the temple, or bowed down and worshipped Satan, He would have fallen for the trap, but Jesus applied the antidote of Scripture. The same is true when we face temptation: The Word of God keeps us from falling for every temptation thrown at us.

Acts as the arsenal of truth: "It is written" (Matthew 4:3-4, 6-7,9-10). The Word of God was a weapon for Jesus just as it is for us. The Bible is meant to be brought out to defend us against the onslaught of deception, strongholds, and crazy ideas that attempt to undermine the work of God in our lives. The Bible is our ammunition for overthrowing spiritual and emotional battles. This is how Jesus confronted and defeated the work of the Enemy, and this is how we must do it.

The priority in Jesus' life was the Word of God. There was a time in Jesus' life when He purposefully planted the Word of God deep in His mind so it would be there to draw out when He needed it. Jesus was so well-versed in Scripture that He was able to spot both the slightest misuse of it and the counterfeit claims made by the Enemy.

> Jesus purposefully planted the Word of God deep in His mind so it would be there to draw out when He needed it.

The Word of God was more than Jesus' devotional material. It was His Bread of Life. He heard His Father in the pages of Scripture. He had left everything to come to earth, but the intimacy He had left behind in heaven was found as He fed on God's Word. We need to see the time we interact with the Word of God as an investment in intimacy.

The time to make these investments is every single day. You don't know what battle you'll find staring you in the face. It will be too late when the next struggle is right upon you. The time to prepare to win is before the drink is offered. The preparation to win out over the temptation to cheat comes before realizing you don't know the answers on a test. Prepare to win over lust before the buttons fly. The daily investment you make in becoming intimate with God's Word will show up when it really counts.

Every time Satan said, "If . . ." Jesus responded with, "It is written." For every lie Satan fired at Him, Jesus had a corresponding truth. How many "It is writtens" do you know? If you were in the desert being tempted by Satan's "Ifs," how many scriptural answers would you come up with? We don't counter lies with more thoughts; we counter them with the Word of God. Not knowing the Word of God will keep us from being effective believers.

Very often I meet students who ask me, "Will you come talk to my friend and help him with a problem?" To which I reply, "Why don't you talk to him yourself?" The students will say, "Well, you know more of the Bible than I do." Then I'll say, "Why do I know more of the Bible than you do?" Of course, there are always different answers given to that question, such things as age or experience. But the reality is that knowing the Bible doesn't come with age. It comes with effort and time spent reading. To be uninformed of Scripture means that we are weaponless, and being weaponless leaves us feeling incapable of speaking to others and helping them in their struggles. Without an arsenal of truth, we are left with our own reasoning, which is of no use in making spiritual progress. Building our arsenal of truth with Scripture places us on the winning side of the battle with the Enemy.

> The daily investment you make in becoming intimate with God's Word will show up when it really counts.

Works as the agent of transformation: "Then the devil left Him" (Matthew 4:11). The process of transformation involves taking out the old and putting in the new. Temptation itself is not a sin, but giving in to it is. Keep in mind that Jesus Himself was tempted but still lived a sinless life. What happens is we are confronted with temptation, which many times leads to desire. Those desires, if not controlled, lead to wrong choices. God's Word is the force that creates new thoughts that lead to a changed life.

God is in the process of transforming you into the image of Jesus Christ. Transformation means change. We can't change ourselves; we must be changed by something. God's Word is the agent of transformation: "Do not be conformed to this world, but be transformed by the renewing of your mind, so that you may prove what the will of God is, that which is good and acceptable and perfect" (Romans 12:2). Every time you are tempted, it's an opportunity for God to lead you past the obstacle and into further personal transformation. God wants you changed into Christ's image, so expect obstacles.

> To be uninformed of Scripture means that we are weaponless, and being weaponless leaves us feeling incapable of speaking to others and helping them in their struggles.

We are fighting an unseen enemy. Our enemy doesn't dig his foxholes in dirt. He digs them in the minds of men. Real progress in the Christian life is made when our thinking starts to change. Our thinking starts to change when we regularly apply the Word of God to our minds. The Word of God is the change agent that produces real transformation.

⑦ UNPACKING THE PASSAGE

1. What was Jesus' physical condition when Satan tempted Him?

2. How many days had Jesus fasted?

3. According to this passage, how many times did Satan tempt Christ?

4. What can you learn from Jesus' example of quoting Scripture in the face of temptation?

5. What does this passage teach about the power of Scripture?

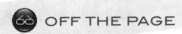

OFF THE PAGE

As strange as it sounds, when it comes to memorizing, we have to train ourselves to remember. Most numbers, addresses, and contact information are stored on our phones or laptops. Just like trying to remember a number that you have never bothered to memorize because it is stored as a contact, there will be times you will need Scripture but will not be able to access the technology to find it; you will have to be able to recall it with your mind. It requires work, but it pays off. Committing Scripture to memory will benefit you in many ways. It will empower you to win in the areas where you face constant struggle. When life goes into panic mode, recalling the Word will give you peace of mind and will release you from intensifying fear and anxiety. When God's Word lives in your thoughts, you will have more courage to share your faith. Placing God's Word deep within your mind will also accelerate your spiritual growth. It will break you out of dangerous life patterns and give you the wisdom to distinguish between the world's truths and lies. Only good can come out of memorizing God's Word.

The temptations Jesus faced can be placed into three groups: emotion, envy, and ego. We face these same kinds of temptations, and it's helpful to have some specific verses memorized to win in these areas of temptation:

- Emotion can tempt us to do something that will put us in a place where God doesn't want us to be.
- Envy can result in using ill means to take what is not ours, resent what others have, or both.
- Ego is an attempt to impress others and ourselves either by being someone we're not or by not humbly giving due credit to God.

We will all face these three temptations in different ways at different times in our lives, usually when we are not expecting it. It's helpful to commit specific verses to memory in order to win over these areas of temptation. Commit the following verses to memory and use them in times of need:

- When *emotion* clouds your thoughts, quote 1 Corinthians 6:19-20.
- When *envy* blinds you to the ways God has blessed you, quote Proverbs 14:30.
- When *ego* causes you to value yourself instead of finding your value in your relationship with Christ, quote Matthew 16:25-26.

PERSONAL DOWNLOAD

Reread Matthew 4:1-11, the chapter's passage. The following questions and suggestions for memorization will help you apply the principle of this chapter to your life and strengthen your journey toward being more like Christ.

1. Describe a time in your life when you struggled with temptation. What steps are you taking to ensure that your arsenal of truth is stocked up?

2. How does this passage reveal the character of Jesus? How does this impact your outlook on temptation?

3. Knowing that Jesus was tempted more than once, how do you plan to deal with the onslaught of temptations that come your way?

4. Why is this passage imperative for Christians to grasp and model?

5. Commit verses 4, 7, and 10 of Matthew 4 to memory. These verses will provide you with specific scriptural truths to deal with the three common human experiences that can sidetrack you from God's purposes. Just think, you'll be quoting the same verses Jesus used in the face of temptation!

//

💬 LIVE THE WORD

At age eighteen, Jeff came home from high school football practice to receive in the mail a letter he had long awaited. It was the letter from a university in Kansas that was offering Jeff a full-ride scholarship to use his skills in football to help take the university all the way to the championship. This is something that not only Jeff had longed for but his entire family as well. As we all know, football is a priority in the great state of Kansas.

As a jock, Jeff found himself being influenced many times by individuals who had anything in mind for Jeff except what was really best for him. Jeff had everything our culture told him he was to have: the crowd, a full-ride football scholarship, a girlfriend he had dated all through high school and was expected to marry. As Jeff was making the transition from being a high school football player with senioritis to up-and-coming university football star, God spoke. He spoke to Jeff in an unmistakable way with a distinct call on his life—and it was not a call to go to the university to play football. God was calling Jeff to be used by God in full-time ministry.

Jeff remembered reading Matthew 4, when Jesus faced his own temptations in the desert. The Enemy had offered Jesus things that would have brought Him momentary satisfaction and would have required Him to give up what God had sent Him to do. Jeff understood the way Jesus must have felt when all the kingdoms of the world were placed at His feet. Jeff knew saying yes to the scholarship would satisfy him emotionally and make him the envy of all his friends, but pursuing football would mean stepping away from what God was calling him to do.

The time had come for Jeff to make a pivotal decision in his life. One decision led to lights, fame, possible trophies, and championship rings; the other led to a small Bible college with professors who would look like anything but professional athletes. Jeff decided on the Bible college even though he knew that his teammates and classmates would question why in the world he would give up so much to settle for what they thought was so little. Jeff recalls how difficult it was to call his recruiting coaches to inform them of his decision to follow God on a path with total uncertainties.

When fall came around, Jeff packed his bags, gathered his items, and placed them in the car. His parents made the trip with him to the small college that would equip him for making an astronomical impact on the lives of students, adults, and leaders around the world. He had successfully fought the temptation to follow worldly pursuits.

Go to www.firstbookchallenge.org to tell us your story about how God and His Word have made a difference in your life, friends, family, school, and church.

//

HEART CHALLENGE

Media, marketers, and salespeople (among others) continue to force-feed false imagery. The businesses that define beauty and success are the same corporations that make the clothing smaller and the prices higher. What a "beautiful" picture of irony. This image-driven culture has led old and young alike to be frustrated with themselves, their anatomy, and their accomplishments. This frustration easily leads to temptation. People are tempted to question their value in personal relationships at school, work, church, and sometimes within their own families. We consistently move through life being bombarded and targeted with temptations, much like Jesus who was bombarded by Satan. Yet every time we see Jesus ward off temptation with the power of Scripture. It is amazing how even the Son of God didn't simply speak to Satan concerning these temptations but also quoted the Word of God.

1. With what temptations do you struggle most?

2. Jesus used Scripture to overcome temptation. What verses do you know of that will best help you overcome temptations you are likely to face? List at least three passages.

3. Overcoming temptation is challenging for even the strongest Christian. The flesh wants what is contrary to the Spirit. This internal battle that continually exists within our lives causes incredible

strife. We can't overcome those challenges and struggles alone; we need friends and leaders around us to encourage us during these trying times. Take a few moments right now to pray that God would put in your heart the names of at least three individuals you could turn to for support. After you've written these names down and God has confirmed this in your life, plan a time to contact each one of these individuals to share what's going on in your life. Ask them to encourage you on this journey.

WRITE COOL STUFF HERE

WRITE COOL STUFF HERE

WRITE COOL STUFF HERE

ALL YOU CAN EAT

🛈 **PRINCIPLE:**
FOR EVERY LIE, THERE IS A TRUTH.

As one of millions of Americans who has spent a significant por-
tion of my life trying to step away from the bread, Jesus saying, "I
am the bread of life" makes me a little nervous. On the one hand,
I think, Oh, of course you are the bread, Lord. You are that warm,
sweet, fluffy, yeasty roll of deliciousness with melting honey-butter
rolling off the top, dropped off at my table by that angel disguised
in the O'Charley's uniform. You are right. You are that glorious slice
of homemade white bread intentionally saved until the end of the
meal — when the roast is gone, and the rice is no more, and all that
is left is a pool of gravy begging to be sopped. I get it, Jesus. You
are definitely the bread. *On the other hand, I think about the love-*
hate relationship I have with carbs and wonder why in the world
Jesus chose to declare Himself bread when there are much health-
ier options from which He could have chosen. Well, why not? After
all, "I am the lettuce of life." Nah, that's too bland. Or maybe, "I am
the grilled chicken breast of life." No, too many vegans. Okay, I
think I've got it: "I am the juicy, seedless watermelon of life."
Perfect! Everyone likes watermelon — at least those with whom I
want to spend eternity. And, anyway, Lord, I get the sense that
watermelon haters also probably reject other pleasures created

by You — such as love, music, and 600-thread-count Egyptian-cotton sheets — so we needn't worry with them.

My problem with the "I am the bread" declaration is that Jesus made this statement two thousand years ago before anyone knew about O'Charley's bread. I hear Jesus' statement through the filter of an American living in the twenty-first century. The role of bread has significantly evolved since Jesus' time. When Jesus declared Himself to be the bread, He was speaking to an audience for which bread was the staple food in their diets. Bread was eaten in the form of flattened rolls and thick buns. It was not necessarily a supplement that added to the meal. For many people, two or three of these buns was their meal. When Christ declared Himself to be the bread of life, He was saying, "I am the staple. I am the thing that sustains you. I am the most fulfilling nourishment for your soul."

///////////

So how does all this bread talk fit into our study of the Bible? Well, let's go back to the gospel of John. John began by writing, "In the beginning was the Word, and the Word was with God, and the Word was God." From the very beginning of his writing, John set up the significance of the Word of God. Understand that every single word, phrase, and sentence written by John was carefully and painstakingly chosen in order to convey the message he had been given by God. It wasn't like John was given an English assignment to write about what it was like to hang with Jesus and then waited until the night before it was due to put something on paper. This wasn't a "What I Did This Summer" essay. This was the mission of John's life. John sat down to write with the intense focus of a man who had been shown the truths of the kingdom of God.

The contents of the book of John are arranged to bring about a thinking conviction that leads to a changed life. The book of John was written seventy years after the resurrection of Christ. Along with his work in the churches and as an eyewitness to the work of Jesus, John knew how lives had been changed by the simple truth that for every lie, there is a truth to fight it.

 **PASSAGE:**
JOHN 8:31-32

> If you abide in My word, you are My disciples indeed. And you shall know the truth, and the truth shall make you free. (NKJV)

If Christ is the Word, as John made clear from the very beginning of his gospel, then we must abide (live) in that Word. *Abide* means "to stay with it." To abide in the Word is to stay in it and continue to read it, no matter how we feel. We choose to believe and act on the Word, regardless of what our emotions tell us, because "truth shall make [us] free."

This is one of the most misused texts in the Bible. Jesus is speaking of continuing in His teaching. In these verses, He is speaking to people who have put their faith in Him as the Messiah and are living their lives from that basis. For these new believers to continue in Jesus' teaching would mark them as genuine disciples and take them into a deeper experience of God's truth. The truth would set them free from the mindset that Christianity was about rules and believing other ideas that have no basis in Scripture. The freedom that Jesus is speaking of is spiritual freedom from sin and its effects. Some of the people listening to Jesus thought He was speaking of political freedom. Everyone has a tendency to define truth and freedom in his or her own terms. These verses relate to the spiritual side of freedom. Jesus is speaking of inner freedom, no longer being under the control of sin. Sin and the secrets we keep break our connection with God. This divide between God and us is caused by both misbelief and destructive desires. The antidote is truth and is found in a restored relationship with Jesus.

It has been said that we should know the truth, but first it will make us miserable. This is an expression of what it takes to get truth into your life. The truth can hurt. A struggle occurs when we open God's Word. It takes on the form of a fight between God's truth and our feelings. The battle wages war on our thoughts and beliefs and invades our actions. Winning the battle to think, believe, and act in accordance with God's Word brings freedom, but be prepared for your emotions and God's truth to collide.

> The truth can hurt. A struggle occurs when we open God's Word. It takes on the form of a fight between God's truth and our feelings.

In John 8:31-32, Jesus reveals three ways of how the truth of God's Word becomes real in our lives. The presence of sin turns everything upside down in our lives. Original sin placed our emotions and appetites in the leadership position and placed God at the bottom. The life, death, and resurrection of Jesus made it possible for us to have our lives turned right-side-up, where we are no longer dominated by sin. The life of Christ can now lead our lives. The strategic element of change is the Word of God. As we read Scripture, we let the weight of God's truth judge our sin and secrets, and the weight of the Word shifts our world right-side-up. In this session, we are going to look at the role the Word of God plays in setting us free.

The Fight for Truth
"If you continue in My word, then you are truly disciples of Mine; and you will know the truth, and the truth will make you free." (John 8:31-32)
The fight for truth is between our emotions and the Word of God. We enter this world led by our emotions. When we're hurt, we cry. When we're hungry, we scream. When we're happy, we laugh. This is normal for children, but too many of us allow our emotions to continue to dictate our adult lives.

God created our emotions to be our sensors. They enable us to enjoy a situation, experience a moment, and interpret danger. Our emotions are the feelers of our lives. They were never meant to lead. Emotions are real, but they are not always right. Unbalanced emotions will always negate your ability to live an abundant and fulfilled life with God. Are you having problems with people or problems with possessions? Guess what? Those are not your problems. You do have a problem — a truth problem! You need more of God's truth in your life. When truth enters a heart that has been led by emotion, emotion will often persuade that heart to believe the opposite of the truth. Here is an example: When someone who has struggled with forgiveness is told, "God has forgiven you and will never bring up your past," he or she responds, "Maybe so, but I still don't feel forgiven." They believe their emotions over truth.

When emotions lead, they justify whatever your mind is thinking. For example, when your mind says, "No one understands you," your emotions justify this by making you feel isolated. When thoughts whisper, "You're the only one who has ever gone through this," emotions kick in by making you feel weird, hopeless, and victimized.

Ladies, maybe you have heard this in your thought life: "That outfit makes you look huge!" Then your emotions punctuate with a chorus of, "What a pig! You'd better just stay behind your desk." Society, family, and well-meaning friends bombard you with thoughts like "You won't be happy until you're married" and "You have to act and look a certain way to fit in." Your emotions take thoughts like these and make you feel desperate and insecure.

> As we read Scripture, we let the weight of God's truth judge our sin and secrets, and the weight of the Word shifts our world right-side-up.

Letting emotions dictate our decisions causes us to misinterpret the events of our lives. When emotions are the lenses through which everything is viewed, it's impossible to get an accurate read on anything. Giving emotions control forces the Word of God to become subjective. Because we have chosen emotions as the basis of reality, we conclude that if we do not feel it, then it must not be real.

The fight for truth depends on reversing emotional control. When the truth of God is planted in your mind, it begins to spread into your habits, actions, and relationships. When you allow the Word of God to take the lead in your life, your emotions obey the truth. Over time you will find that your life takes on a healthy emotional balance because truth has won the fight and you are no longer a wacko!

The Framework of Truth
"You will know the truth." (John 8:32)

The truth is God's Word, not what people say about God's Word or what you read in the tabloids about God's Word. Truth is the Spirit-breathed Word of God. The Word of God is the basis for our faith. The Word gives us the faith we need. Faith, in turn, helps us overcome whatever we face. The Word of God is the framework on which our thoughts are based. It is the basis for the ethics of our lives. You have been given the privilege to know the truth and to be free. The word *know* in this verse means that you can live out the Word of God every day with the highest conviction and belief that you have confidently chosen that which is right.

> When the truth of God is planted in your mind, it begins to spread into your habits, actions, and relationships.

The Word of God is designed to bring clarity into our cluttered thoughts. This verse uses the word *know* in relation to the truth. We have to do more than just glance at verses. We have to take them off the page and download them into our thoughts.

The Function of Truth
"The truth will make you free." (John 8:32)

The function of truth is to make you free. Anyplace in our lives we believe a lie is a place where the truth is not. The place we find ourselves in bondage to destructive behavior is a place where truth needs to be applied. Where there is truth, there is freedom — freedom to live the full and meaningful life Jesus promised. For the truth to free us, we must make an intentional choice to begin the process of renewing our minds. The process is simple; the journey is not. The process begins when we recognize a lie and respond with the truth. The thoughts we think and the emotions attached to those thoughts can be counterbalanced with the truth.

Something is going to shape our lives. We get to choose. It will be either the lies we've grown up believing, the messages of the world, or the truth of God.

Consider the following lies (THINK) and compare them to God's truth (BELIEVE). Then write the Scriptures in your own words (ACT).

"FOR EVERY LIE, THERE'S A CORRESPONDING TRUTH."

THINK	BELIEVE	ACT
"It's too late for me to start over."	Psalm 138:8	
"I have a right to get even."	Romans 12:17	
"I can do it myself. No one will tell me what to do."	Psalm 118:6,9	
"You gotta do what it takes to fit in."	Proverbs 13:20	

THINK	BELIEVE	ACT
"Not even God can get me out of this one."	Romans 8:28	
"I can't."	Philippians 4:13	
"It's my life. I'll do what I want to."	Proverbs 3:5-6	
"I can't help it. It's just the way I am."	2 Corinthians 10:5	
"My life is one big mistake."	Psalm 139:14-15	
"Character doesn't matter."	Proverbs 10:9	

These and many other verses throughout Scripture serve as our most powerful weapons against temptation. Choose the ones that benefit you the most. Write them on index cards. Carry the cards with you. Begin the process of memorizing them, meditating on them, and speaking them aloud in specific situations that call for specific truths. With practice, these powerful weapons become lethal to temptation.

It's good to know that it's not too late to begin the process of renewing our minds with the Word of God. You might have found the previous verses to be helpful, but that's not all the Bible has to say to you.

Make daily Bible reading a habit. Allow God's Word to be "mental floss" that gets to those hard-to-reach places to root out the lies you have chosen to believe. Allow God's Word to transform your mind. As you do, you will find that the truth is renewing your thoughts, your words, and ultimately your choices.

Factoid: It takes about twenty-one days of doing something before it becomes a habit.

 UNPACKING THE PASSAGE

1. To whom is Jesus speaking in this passage?

2. What teaching is Jesus referring to in verse 31?

3. How does this passage say that you will know the truth?

4. According to this passage, what is required to be set free?

5. What does it mean to be a disciple of Christ?

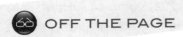

OFF THE PAGE

There are no new thoughts. If you have thought it, the Bible talks about it. For every lie, Scripture supplies a corresponding truth. Everyone battles his or her thoughts. It is often hard to figure out what to do with them. The best thing to do is to begin thinking about what you are thinking about. For example, when you act out in a negative way, what thoughts are going through your head? When you are stressed, depressed, doubtful, or in despair, what are you thinking? Next time you feel nervous or afraid, look up your feelings on biblegateway.com. Find a verse that gives you hope about being nervous or afraid, and then commit it to memory.

Every time you have a thought that triggers a negative action or causes you to have a meltdown, write that thought down and then use an online concordance to look up the different words in that thought. If you have a Bible with a concordance in the back of it, all the words of Scripture are arranged alphabetically. Flip to the concordance and look up the words that describe what you are dealing with at that moment. For instance, if what you are feeling is anger, flip to the beginning and look up the word *anger*. Read all the verses listed until you find one that gives you hope. Then download it to your memory.

PERSONAL DOWNLOAD

Reread John 8:31-32, the chapter's passage. The following questions and suggestions for memorization will help you apply the principle of this chapter to your life and strengthen your journey toward being more like Christ.

1. Describe the difference between *feeling* that something is right or wrong and *knowing* something is right or wrong. When have you allowed your emotions to lead you rather than you leading your emotions?

2. How does knowing the principle "For every lie, there is a truth" affect the importance of reading the Bible?

3. Describe one area in your life that has been holding you back from experiencing true freedom in Christ. Ask God to show you the truth regarding that area and set you free from that stronghold.

4. Have you ever doubted your relationship with Christ? If so, how has this study helped you trust in it?

5. Commit John 8:32 to memory. This verse will remind you to measure your thoughts, beliefs, and actions against God's truth.

///

💬 LIVE THE WORD

Dominant thoughts in student culture demand, "Me first. If I want it, I'll get it. I want to show everybody how great I am." These thoughts are so ingrained in our lives that they go unchallenged until they come in contact with God's Word. Scripture teaches putting others first, particularly the "least of these." Selfish thoughts begin to lose their hold as God's Spirit of servanthood takes over. It is at this point that we are set free from the influences of our culture and society.

Every year in South Florida during the Christmas season, a group of individuals gathers to demonstrate what putting others first actually looks like. These students model the very heart of John 8:31-32. By submitting their lives to Christ and reflecting on what it means to be a true follower of Jesus, these students have had a change of mind. They have been set free from their old self-image and replaced it with a freedom to reach out to others. Amid trouble, pain, and suffering in this community, students assemble every year to demonstrate what it looks like to reach out with Christ's love. Instead of focusing on whether or not their parents purchased all the items on their personal Christmas lists, these students provide food, clothing, gifts, and toys to struggling families. They don't drop gifts off at doorsteps and shelters; they knock on hundreds of doors. And when those doors open, the students stand ready with smiling faces and boxes packed with all the food, clothing, gifts, and toys to make Christmas special for the family across the threshold. The recipients not only accept boxes of goods but they receive the message that somebody loves and cares for them. They see the pages of Scripture come to life, and they experience God's love.

Go to www.firstbookchallenge.org to tell us your story about how God and His Word have made a difference in your life, friends, family, school, and church.

///

 ## HEART CHALLENGE

Service requires sacrifice. Many times we must sacrifice the things we want in order to continue along our journey with Christ. This means putting the truths of Scripture into practice. When we do this, we move from simply doing things to becoming more like Christ. When we put truth into practice, we are freed from the false images and temptations of our culture. We are strengthened to live and share this truth with others.

1. When you look at your heart, do you see a passion to become all God created you to be? Please explain.

2. How does culture depict service? Which is more prevalent in the media: serving or being served? Can you think of a specific example?

3. How does Scripture depict service? How does the Bible describe the freedom found in releasing our desires over to God and following His desires to impact others? What does this look like?

4. List a person, family, organization, or community to which you can model what it looks like to experience God's transformation — not based on emotions but on the truth of Scripture. How will you specifically demonstrate God's transforming power?

WRITE COOL STUFF HERE

WRITE **COOL** STUFF HERE

CHAPTER 4

OXYGEN FOR THE SOUL

PRINCIPLE:
BREATHING IN GOD'S WORD
BRINGS LIFE TO OUR SPIRITS.

Most know what it's like to have been forced to read a really boring book. I had a professor in college who insisted his students read Beowulf *in its original form, which he claimed was some early version of English. (I think what he meant by "early version of English" was that* Beowulf *was written by a German toddler.) As hard as I tried, I could not make heads or tails out of this epic literary work. I had to watch the movie to figure out that when the poem says that the dragon had a Danish for breakfast, the writer didn't really mean that the dragon liked delicious jelly-filled pastries. And imagine my horror when the chubby grandmotherly lady from Denmark got her head chomped off like a marshmallow Peep. Needless to say, the unit test on* Beowulf *was not my most shining academic moment. Because I could not understand the language of* Beowulf, *the story meant nothing to me. I could barely stay awake as we read it in class. The words were dead. Because there was no point of reference for me, I could not connect with the text.*

For years I had the same trouble when it came to reading the Bible. God's living Word was dead to me because I did not know how to make it relevant. I didn't know how to take what I read and find truths that could be downloaded into my everyday life. I did not know how to make the Word come alive.

//////////////

The Bible declares that all Scripture is God-breathed. Although the Bible was written with human hands and spoken through human mouths, it was God who breathed each verse into being and made the Bible a living book. The Bible is the living Word, breathed into existence by the living God. This is the meaning of inspiration: God exhales His Word and we inhale the life it provides. When we read Scripture, we read God-breathed words. The Spirit of God brings the words to life in us. It may seem obvious, but it is possible to study the text, learn about the background, discover meanings of words, and still see lifeless words. The Spirit of God is necessary to help us understand the Bible. Without the Holy Spirit, reading Scripture is a lifeless act.

The breath of God that inspired Scripture also inspires us, becoming a creative and productive Word in our lives. God breathes on the text, we breathe it in, and a unique connection occurs. The Spirit creates an encounter between the writer, the reader, and God, who is living, active, and piercing.

> All Scripture is God-breathed, meaning that God brought it into being and breathes it into us as we read it.

Paul's second letter to Timothy explains that all Scripture is God-breathed, meaning that God brought it into being and breathes it into us as we read it. Every word of Scripture came directly from the mouth of the Lord. He spoke it. He breathed into the writers and prophets and onto the page.

Timothy was a second-generation Christian who, as a child, had been taught the Scriptures by his grandmother and his mother. He grew up knowing the stories of the Bible. They fueled his imagination. His heroes had always been the people of Scripture. God's Word had inspired, comforted, and motivated him. But that was the Scripture of his childhood; now things were different. As a young man, Timothy was the pastor of the church in Ephesus. This city was rapidly changing for the worse. There was political chaos and social crisis. The city was full of corruption, false worship, and extreme indifference toward God. Timothy's church was feeling the impact of the atmosphere of the city. The church at Ephesus had also come under personal attack from a jealous religious system. For Timothy, there was much to fear. Living in such uncertain times called for real solutions of which Timothy was unsure how to find.

Paul, who had been Timothy's mentor, reached out to him through his letters. This letter of 2 Timothy was written one week before Paul died. Paul knew what he was talking about. He had lived and ministered in extreme circumstances of discomfort. For the sake of the gospel, he had suffered physically and emotionally. He had challenged political systems, confronted religious leaders, and called followers of Christ to remain faithful. Paul was a man who was not afraid of a challenge. He had faced every circumstance head-on. He considered the afflictions he encountered a small price to pay in order to see the kingdom of God be made known on the earth. His intense zeal and driving passion to extend the work of God did not come out of his own ability. His roots were in the Word of God. Without a doubt, Paul's understanding of Scripture was completely revolutionized after his conversion. He had grown up reading and observing the commands of Scripture religiously, but it was not until his encounter with Christ on the road to Damascus that Scripture unfolded in a whole new way. The Holy Spirit taught him that all the promises and prophecies of the Old Testament pointed to Jesus. Paul had discovered that God's Word was alive with His breath.

PASSAGE:
2 TIMOTHY 3:14-17

You, however, continue in the things you have learned and become convinced of, knowing from whom you have learned them, and that from childhood you have known the sacred writings which are able to give you the wisdom that leads to salvation through faith which is in Christ Jesus. All Scripture is inspired by God and profitable for teaching, for reproof, for correction, for training in righteousness; so that the man of God may be adequate, equipped for every good work.

Paul challenged Timothy to hold on to God's Word because it gives clarity, direction, and vitality of life. Timothy lived in a city that was suffocating spiritually. Paul told Timothy not to get caught up in all the turmoil of the city but to draw breath from the Word of God, as it is inspired by God and productive in every part of life. Paul did not present the Bible as theory but declared the Scripture in Timothy's possession to be alive with the breath of God and full of the transforming information that this young disciple needed in his life of faith. The Bible was for Timothy—as it is for all of us—the source to know the love of God in Jesus Christ and develop in us a saving relationship. Although Timothy had known the Scripture religiously as a child, he experienced a reawakening of it.

The Bible is not merely a work of humans but the Word of God. We must choose to accept its principles and walk in God's practices. We want to move beyond knowing the facts of the text to hearing God's Word in the text. The Bible begins with the activity of God. The words are His and exist so we can hear Him speak. They are effective only when we approach them in a spirit of openness and faith.

> God's Word is oxygen for our spirits. Just as we cannot physically live without breathing, our souls cannot live without the oxygen of God's Word.

Remember a time you felt as if you were going to lose your breath and started to panic. Your body is programmed for the active movement of breathing, a combination of inhaling and exhaling. Your body memorizes this process internally and in its perfect working order causes you to breathe naturally.

Just as our physical bodies exist by breathing, our spiritual lives require the same breathing movements. Breathing, whether physical or spiritual, requires two responses: inhaling and exhaling. Without breathing, your body would never get the oxygen it needs and would suffer, shut down, and then die. Likewise, God's Word is oxygen for our spirits. Just as we cannot physically live without breathing, our souls cannot live without the oxygen of God's Word. Think of reading the Bible as inhaling God's Word into our lives and exhaling the effect of His Word as we live it out in our relationships. The following describes four specific benefits of breathing God's Word, all of which are found in 2 Timothy 3:14-17.

1. Leads us in how to live. God-breathed Scripture is **profitable for teaching**. This teaching has a specific goal in mind: to bring us into an encounter with the gospel of Jesus. The word *teach* in this verse means to explain. This refers not to the method of teaching but to the content. The Bible teaches us the content of Christianity by painting pictures in the Old Testament and teaching principles in the New Testament. God-breathed Scripture gives us the most complete work of truth necessary for living, serving, and witnessing.

2. Keeps us from drifting from God. God-breathed Scripture brings **reproof**. *Reproof* means to discipline or correct in a sharp way. Getting at the heart of why we do what we do and what drives us to destructive behavior is the focus of being reproved by Scripture. Most Christians, while reading the Bible, have experienced times of being convicted of unhealthy choices and ungodly beliefs. The Holy Spirit uses God's Word to tear down false ideas and build new life-giving beliefs into our thoughts. God helps us sort truth from lies, negative thoughts from positive thoughts, good intentions from bad intentions, and points us to where He intends our lives to be.

3. Brings clarity into our choices. God-breathed Scripture brings **correction**. The word *correction* means to straighten out the crooked. God takes the areas of our lives that are bent and aligns them to His purpose. He challenges us to obey. He shows us what is right and gives us the ability to do it. Here *correction* refers to restoration — setting something back up that has fallen down. Where there has been reproof, the Word of God builds us up by replacing lies with truth.

4. Helps us to know what is right. God-breathed Scripture provides **training in righteousness**. The word *training* means to nurture, educate, and instruct us. The word *righteousness* means right standing with God. Breathing in God's Word and knowing how to live life God's way matures us into being fully functioning followers of Jesus Christ. As we continue to strengthen our understanding of the Word, we find ourselves with a clearer understanding of what is right and what is wrong. That is not to say that we have it all figured out. However, this passage encourages us to consistently be in a training mindset. *Training* implies that something is done over and over with the goal being improvement. As we study the Word, we will be trained and strengthened to live righteous lives.

> When we are full of the breath of God, we become "adequate, equipped for every good work" (2 Timothy 3:17).

We must continually breathe in and out these four benefits. When we are full of the breath of God, we become "adequate, equipped for every good work" (2 Timothy 3:17). When we read Scripture, God reveals who Jesus is, what truth is, how to do the right thing, and why it is imperative to allow God's Word to continually inspire us through His Spirit.

UNPACKING THE PASSAGE

1. What does this passage teach you about God's Word?

2. What does it mean that Scripture is "God-breathed"?

3. This passage says that Scripture is useful for what?

4. This passage says that Scripture will equip you for what?

5. According to this passage, what has God shaped you to accomplish?

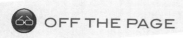 OFF THE PAGE

You have probably already asked yourself, *How do you do it? How do you read the Word and breathe in the breath of God?* What follows are some suggestions on how to breathe spiritually.

To breathe spiritually, you must stay in the moment.
Some people have called it "short-attention-span Bible reading." This is when you begin to read your Bible and then realize that a YouTube clip or annoying song lyrics are running through your head. You've been looking at the same page for two minutes, but your mind is somewhere else. When this happens, readjust your focus. Read the verses again and again until you can clearly refocus on the passage. This will help you stay in the moment and in the Word.

To breathe spiritually, read for transformation, not just information.
We are all faced with complex issues, major choices, multiple responsi-bilities at home and school, options with our free time, and concerns

about relationships. Lay these issues, decisions, and concerns before the text. Give God access to all areas of your life by saying, *God, I'm here. Speak to me about any and every part of my life. I want to be a life that reflects Your love and grace. Turn me into the person You want me to be.*

To breathe spiritually, remember that less is more.

Instead of reading massive amounts of Scripture, first let what you have already read filter into all the places of your soul. Having fewer verses applied is better than a lot of verses skimmed and then forgotten.

No matter how much of the Bible you read, there will always be more of God's Word to experience. Assuming that you understand Scripture simply because you know the stories in the Bible will cause you to miss out on new insight. Accumulating facts about Scripture is not the same as knowing the God of Scripture. Knowing God is a relational experience. We experience Scripture by inhaling it into our spirit and exhaling it into our lives. For example, we breathe in John 13:34, which says, "A new commandment I give to you, that you love one another, even as I have loved you, that you also love one another." We breathe out physical actions of love to others. We choose not to be irritated with family, judge our friends, or keep people at a distance because of our superior (or inferior) attitudes.

Allowing John 13:34 to impact how you deal with people causes you to replace your old relationship patterns with the way Christ loved others. When you breathe in Scripture, the Spirit takes those words and moves them from your head into specific areas of your life. As you read Scripture, the Spirit will help you understand what you are reading and what you can do to allow it to become oxygen to your life.

Ask questions of the text you are reading. Here are three questions you can ask of any passage of Scripture:

1. How does this impact my relationship with God and with others?
Too often we never connect the verses we read with our relationships. In what relationship can you live out the truths revealed?

2. **Why would you not live out this truth?** Make a list of excuses for not obeying this Scripture. Push back at the text. For example, in response to Jesus' words in John to love each other, you may say, "Well, I will love them, but I won't like them." We use objections when we don't want to obey Scripture. What might be the result of *not* obeying God's Word?

3. **What are you going to do with it?** To get to the take-away of the verse, it's helpful to pray the Scripture to God. Doing this will make the text more personal. God will answer the Scripture that you pray. When it comes to loving others, you may pray the words of John 13:34, "Dear God, You've given me a command to love others in all the ways You've loved others. I know this has not always been true of how I've treated people. Create in me the capacity to be sensitive to those who are hurting around me. Amen."

PERSONAL DOWNLOAD

Reread 2 Timothy 3:14-17, the chapter's passage. The following questions and suggestions for memorization will help you apply the principle of this chapter to your life and strengthen your journey toward being more like Christ.

1. What is the difference between knowing the Word of God and knowing the God of the Word?

2. What are the biggest hindrances to your reading the Bible? (Listing specific distractions will help you avoid them the next time you read God's Word.)

3. In what way does this passage give you hope?

4. How does thinking of God's Word as oxygen change your view of Scripture?

5. Commit 2 Timothy 3:16-17 to memory. These verses will remind you of the divine source of the Bible and its incredible benefits.

///

💬 LIVE THE WORD

Maria was a junior in high school who was dealing with heavy pressures. The majority of her friends and family had no idea the challenges and struggles she was facing. Maria was like most students. She attended her youth group with a smile on her face. She had great parents and a loving home. Her family drove top-of-the-line vehicles. She excelled academically. She had a boyfriend, a place on the cheerleading squad, and a spot on the gymnastics team. All in all, Maria appeared to be like everyone else. But most people weren't aware of her internal struggle. She dealt with an unbearable load of pressure to excel. The pressure became so painful and emotional that it began to affect her spiritually and physically. She described her life in a letter.

She wrote that she saw herself as a young lady carrying a backpack of rocks. Each rock represented a different pressure and struggle she was dealing with. The rocks of academic pressure and stipulations from her boyfriend to be sexually involved in their relationship grew heavier and heavier. She reiterated that her youth group had no idea of the internal issues with which she struggled. She felt she could not openly share what she was going through for fear of being ridiculed and judged on a religious level. She feared not measuring up to the spiritual level where everyone had placed her.

Pressure on top of pressure added tremendous weight to her pack. Maria described her pack weighing so much that it cut into her shoulders, to the point that she bled as she moved through life. She described her life not as a field of flowers, a bustling school campus, or a safe and happy family around the dinner table but as a wet, damp, black tunnel. She concluded her letter by saying, "At the end of the day, I am there alone in the black tunnel with no end in sight and there is no light to be seen."

That's it. That is the way the letter ends. The comfort, encouragement, and strength Maria needed to deal with the pressures of life are found in God's Word. Just like Maria could have, we can draw breath for life from Scripture and experience God's peace and security.

Go to www.firstbookchallenge.org to tell us your story about how God and His Word have made a difference in your life, friends, family, school, and church.

///

 ## HEART CHALLENGE

God desires to provide you with all you need to function in the way He designed you to live. In the presence of the everyday pressures of life, He offers peace in a way that you've never encountered before. Because

He loves you, God wants to take off the weight of your life's pack so you can demonstrate that same love to others.

1. What are the toughest challenges and pressures you are experiencing right now?

2. How have these pressures affected your life physically? How has your relationship with God been impacted?

3. Ask God to speak to you in a way that He's never spoken to you before. Open up your heart, mind, and soul to listen to what He has to say. Embrace God's encouragement and peace. Trust Him and His Word.

WRITE **COOL** STUFF HERE

WRITE COOL STUFF HERE

CONCLUSION

There is more to spiritual transformation than the simple maturity of our outward appearance and coordinated religious expressions. True transformation invites us to experience the rush of God's Word, connecting us to our Creator and allowing us to experience Him in our thoughts, emotions, and personality.

When we download Scripture into our personal DNA, we are able to apply and understand God's Word prior to going out and living it. We do this when we read the Bible systematically and record specific details and truths that the Holy Spirit brings to mind. Our understanding of Scripture grows and we become more sensitive to the Holy Spirit's guidance and work in our lives.

We have many opportunities to reflect on the transformation that has or has not taken place in our lives. As we encounter struggles and temptations, God provides His arsenal of truth that will stand against the temptations of our culture. Our spiritual weapon of quoting Scripture causes us to advance against the Enemy.

We must wrestle with whether or not we will truly believe the truths of Scripture — not simply comprehending God's Word in our minds but allowing God's Word to be reflected in our actions. Internal transformation screams to be believed and used. This revelation is evident in our lives when we give God permission to live out loud with our daily actions.

The strength we find in His Word enables us to overcome the challenges of life and it gives life renewed focus. We begin to take on life with a confidence that communicates more than emotional transition but a reflection of spiritual transformation through God.

When we possess not only the knowledge but also the power of His anointing through Scripture, we are propelled to make God's Book the First Book in our minds, thoughts, emotions, and lives.

BE A BETTER BIBLE READER

1. As you read Scripture, make a mental picture of what is going on in the text.
2. Highlight verses, words, and phrases that stand out to you. Often these serve as indicators that the Spirit of God wants to speak to you about these things.
3. Every time you eat or drink, make it a point to look at the verse you read earlier that day. This is where technology, sticky notes, and note cards come in handy.
4. Work what you've read into a conversation with others, perhaps by restating the verse. You might say, "I read something about that the other day." Talking about what you have read will make you recall it, which will help you learn it.
5. Approach Scripture with a flexible mind and an open heart. Don't assume you know everything about what you are preparing to read. As you read God's Word, you will realize how much more you need to know.
6. Read Scripture to encounter God. Let the verses lead you to a deeper insight than you could experience on your own.
7. Read Scripture every day. The depth of your experience will be in direct proportion to the amount of attention you give God's Word. There is no substitute for reading Scripture. Use online resources such as Bible dictionaries, commentaries, and encyclopedias. Remember that although these tools can assist you in your understanding of Scripture, there is nothing that can take the place of *reading* it.

8. Write down questions you have after reading God's Word. Next time you read Scripture, these questions will direct you to what you are looking for.

9. Don't be afraid to take on big topics in Scripture such as sin, suffering, and the uniqueness of the deity of Christ. Have confidence that as you study His Word, God will speak to you.

10. Remember that you need the Spirit's help when reading the Bible. Reading without the Spirit's help won't do much for you. It's God's Spirit that shapes your character and your service to others.

11. Restate the verses as a status update —140 characters or less. Distilling a verse down to Twitter-sized chunks helps clarify the meaning so you can carry it with you.

PASSING ON THE FIRST BOOK CHALLENGE:

CARRY IT. LIVE IT. GIVE IT.

You can be a great Christian — if you are willing to pay the price. To pursue greatness in Christianity means to be willing to turn your life of faith into an *intentional* pursuit. Being intentional means making choices based on God and the priority of His Word. Living your faith on purpose means that you begin to let the relationship you have with God and the knowledge of His Word influence all your decisions and your relationships with others. Being intentional means that you've decided it's worth it to invest in your spiritual life as well as help others with their spiritual lives.

Inside every person is a great believer waiting to be unleashed. Most students have found that they make more progress as a disciple when helping someone else do the same. Investing spiritually in the lives of others is an amazing experience. Now that you have journeyed through this phase of First Book Challenge — learning skills for reading and recalling the Word and having a deeper understanding of what a Spirit-led life looks like — take the First Book pledge.

THE FIRST BOOK PLEDGE

You have completed your journey through this phase of the First Book Challenge, but your journey is not over. Your relationship with God continues to develop. Take the First Book Challenge a step further:

- Be a change agent on your campus.
- Lead at least one person through these four sessions.
- Carry your Bible with you every day.
- Be intentional about how you live.
- Give one of your friends a Bible.

Will you take the First Book Challenge? Sign your name below to indicate that you pledge to make God's Word the first book you turn to in your life.

_____

signature   date

You are wired to make a difference. Whenever God's Book becomes the First Book, great things happen! You can find additional resources for First Book Challenge at www.firstbookchallenge.org.

ABOUT THE AUTHORS

DAVID EDWARDS has launched seven citywide, multi-church Bible studies for high school students, which have ranged in attendance from 200 to 1,600. He is a friend of the local church and pastors and is a supporter of Intelligent Youth Ministry.

David connects Scripture to students and their culture, while helping leaders and parents connect to the next generation. He masterfully applies biblical truths to current issues in an honest, humorous, and understandable form. His mission is to reintroduce the truth of God's Word by meeting people where they are in life and bringing them one step closer to knowing and becoming like Jesus Christ.

David has authored nineteen books. He travels and speaks more than three hundred times a year for churches, camps, retreats, and leadership meetings. For more information, connect with David at DaveTown.com.

JOHN STAMPER speaks and writes nationally to audiences of all ages. However, he has a special heart to see students rise up and take a leadership role in their families, schools, and churches. Over the past fifteen years, John has been dedicated as a pastor to teach, disciple, and mentor students and families through churches, schools, camps, sporting events, and community organizations. He has the unique ability to connect with all ages, enlightening and motivating individuals to follow Christ and connect to His Word. For more information, connect with John at johnstamper.info.

Other books in the
First Book Challenge series!

The Message: First Book Challenge Edition
Eugene H. Peterson

You're learning how to read and study the Bible — why not learn to understand it better with *The Message*? Written in contemporary language, the way you speak to a friend, *The Message* is easy to read and understand for any age.

978-1-61747-833-8

Available now!

VAST
978-1-61521-914-8

Coming soon!

BOOST
978-1-61747-167-4

MY LIFE IS **TOUGHER** THAN MOST **PEOPLE REALIZE.**

I TRY TO KEEP EVERYTHING *IN BALANCE:* FRIENDS, FAMILY, WORK, SCHOOL, AND GOD.

IT'S NOT EASY.

I KNOW WHAT MY PARENTS BELIEVE AND WHAT MY PASTOR SAYS.

BUT IT'S NOT ABOUT THEM. IT'S ABOUT ME...

ISN'T IT TIME I OWN MY FAITH?

THROUGH THICK AND THIN, KEEP YOUR HEARTS AT ATTENTION, IN ADORATION BEFORE CHRIST, YOUR MASTER. BE READY TO SPEAK UP AND TELL ANYONE WHO ASKS WHY YOU'RE LIVING THE WAY YOU ARE, AND ALWAYS WITH THE UTMOST COURTESY. 1 PETER 3:15 (MSG)

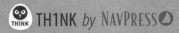
www.navpress.com | 1-800-366-7788   THINK   TH1NK *by* NAVPRESS

PERFECT for **Wednesday nights** or **weekend retreats**!

JUSTLIKECHRIST
GET EVERYTHING YOU NEED WITH THESE BOX SETS.

∨
∨ Full of vibrant, colorful pages, these four-week studies are filled with dynamic group activities, Bible study questions, and a memory verse each week for the students. Each box contains 10 student books, a DVD, and a web license (includes your teaching lessons).

∨
∨ These pocket-sized devotional journals help students engage in God's Word day by day.

[
JustLikeChrist studies allow students to dig deeper in God's Word and relate the Bible to real life. Teachers and leaders access the lessons through an online delivery system.
]

FOR MORE INFORMATION, call **1-888-811-9934**
or go online to **JustLikeChrist.com.**

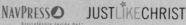
NAVPRESS○   JUSTLIKECHRIST

The Message Means Understanding

Bringing the Bible to all ages

*T*he Message is written in contemporary language that is much like talking with a good friend. When paired with your favorite Bible study, *The Message* will deliver a reading experience that is reliable, energetic, and amazingly fresh.

HELPING STUDENTS
KNOW CHRIST
THROUGH
HIS WORD

What will YOUR STUDENTS do this summer?

Choose from TWO great options.

STUDENT LIFE CAMP

- Engaging worship from experienced worship leaders

- Learning through sound biblical teaching and Bible study

- Community in family groups

- Freedom for you to focus on your students

STUDENT LIFE MISSION CAMP

- Repairing homes, landscaping, painting, and other work projects

- Serving food, organizing donations, and helping at homeless shelters

- Visiting nursing homes and mental health centers

- Leading children's activities and teaching Bible stories to children

For more information on Student Life Camps and Mission Camps, go to **studentlife.com** or call **1-800-718-2267**.